Disney

Classic
Storybook
Collection

GO BACK

Disney PRESS

LOS ANGELES • NEW YORK

Contents

SUSTAINABLE FORESTRY INITIATIVE **Certified Sourcing**
www.sfiprogram.org
SFI-01268

This Label Applies to Text Stock Only

Disney
Lilo & Stitch

The Dog Show

In the middle of the Pacific Ocean, on the little island of Kauai, there lived a girl named Lilo and her pet, Stitch. Lilo was no ordinary girl. She loved doing everything her own way. And Stitch was no ordinary pet. He was an alien from outer space!

Every weekend, Lilo went to a dance class with the other girls from her town, while Stitch waited patiently outside. But today was different. Today there was another pet waiting outside with Stitch.

When dance class was over, Lilo's classmate Myrtle introduced Lilo and Stitch to her new dog. "Her name is Cashmere. She's a purebred poodle." Myrtle scowled down at Stitch, who was eating a scoop of ice cream off the sidewalk. "Breeding is so important when it comes to pets," she said.

Lilo was embarrassed. She tried to ignore the mean things Myrtle said to her and Stitch, but it wasn't easy. "Stitch might not be like other dogs, but he's really smart!" Lilo said.

Just then, Stitch started rolling around in the melted ice cream.

"If Stitch is so smart," Myrtle said, "prove it." She handed Lilo a flyer. "There's a dog show next weekend. Cashmere and I are planning to win, and we'd love to beat you and Stitch."

Myrtle waved as she and Cashmere strutted away.

Lilo and Stitch both growled, and Lilo crumbled the flyer into a tight ball.

Stitch nuzzled against Lilo. He glanced around to see if anyone could hear him. "Bully," he said.

But Lilo was already smoothing out the dog show flyer. "I'm tired of Myrtle being mean to us. Let's show her and Cashmere what we can do, Stitch!"

Stitch loked at Lilo and then nodded. "For Lilo."

The next weekend, Lilo and Stitch showed up at the dog show. They were ready. At least, they hoped they were. But as the judges led everyone into the ring, Lilo started to get nervous. She was glad her sister, Nani, had come along to cheer them on.

"Welcome, everyone," a friendly man with a microphone announced. "Let's start the show with a classic." The man gestured to a row of hoops. "Whichever dog can clear these hoops the fastest will win this round. Up first: Lilo and her dog, Stitch!"

Lilo sized up the rings. It would be a tight fit, but she was sure Stitch could zoom through them.

"Go, Stitch. Go!" Lilo shouted. Stitch took a deep breath and then ran toward the rings. He grabbed the first ring . . . and immediately shoved it in his mouth. He managed to swallow it whole and then chomped down the next four rings. He ran happily back to Lilo and whispered, "Clear!"

"No, Stitch," Lilo sighed. "You were supposed to jump through the rings."

Stitch's ears drooped. "Sorry." He burped and then looked back at the shocked audience.

"Well, that's one way to clear the rings," the man with the microphone said. "It's a good thing we have some extra rings for our next contestants!"

Soon the extra rings were set up. Cashmere sped through them and happily bounded back to Myrtle.

"It's okay, Stitch," Lilo said. "We have two events left. We can still win!" Stitch nodded eagerly.

"On to the next challenge," the man with the microphone shouted as the judges placed three tubes in a zigzag shape on the ground. "In order to complete this event, each dog must run through the three tubes to get to the other side of the course!"

Lilo and Stitch were up first again. "I know you can do this, Stitch," Lilo said. "Just try not to eat anything."

Lilo took a step back and held her breath. She crossed her fingers that Stitch would do well at this challenge.

Stitch licked Lilo playfully and got into position.

"Ready. Set. Go!" the man with the microphone yelled.

Like a bullet, Stitch shot out from the starting line and ran toward the first tunnel. But instead of running inside the tubes, the powerful alien smashed through the sides of each one, running in a straight line from one side of the course to the other.

Stitch crossed the finish line and looked back at the judges proudly. Then he saw Lilo covering her face. Stitch hung his head. He knew he must have done something wrong.

"It's okay. Come here, boy," Lilo called to Stitch.

When Stitch reached her, Lilo said, "I don't think they're going to give us any points for that one, but we still have one event left."

Stitch watched as Cashmere easily navigated the extra tubes. She and Myrtle had so many points, there was no way for Lilo and Stitch to win now.

The last challenge was to cross a balance beam. "They don't have an extra balance beam, so you'll have to go last," Myrtle told Lilo.

Lilo wanted to say something mean back to Myrtle, but she took a deep breath instead. "Good luck, Cashmere," she said through gritted teeth.

Lilo watched as Cashmere crossed the balance beam. She was perfect. One of the judges even said she'd never seen a dog with more poise.

But Lilo was not ready to give up. She knew that Stitch was a talented pet and that he could be just as poised as Cashmere. Lilo and Stitch waited for every other dog to cross the beam. Finally, it was Stitch's turn.

"Okay, Stitch. Run as fast as you can!" Lilo said.

Stitch nodded and raced across the beam. One quick hop and he was already halfway across the thin platform. He turned back to smile at Lilo. But as he did, he tripped on the beam. Stitch scratched at the side of the beam. Most dogs would have fallen off the side, but Stitch was no dog. He used his alien arms to keep crawling along the bottom of the beam instead!

The crowd gasped as Stitch dismounted on the other side.

"I think we'd better go," Lilo said quickly.

Lilo ran to Nani and asked her to take them home.

"Don't you want to stay for the results?" Nani asked.

Lilo shook her head. "No. I think we all know who's going to win." She watched as one of the judges rushed to shake Myrtle's hand.

Stitch whimpered beside Lilo. He felt bad for not doing better at the show.

"It's okay, Stitch," Lilo said. "It was my fault. I should have given better instructions."

Nani watched as Lilo hugged Stitch.

That night, Nani pulled out two large, flat rocks wrapped in shiny tinfoil. "I made you these. They're supposed to be medals," she said, blushing.

On the backs, Nani had written their names and the words MOST CREATIVE. "You did finish all the challenges. You just did them in your own way."

"Thank you, Nani," Lilo said, giving her sister a hug.

"Yes, thanks for Nani," Stitch said, joining the hug. He might not have won the dog show, but he had something even better: a family that loved him no matter what!

A Snack for the Queen

It was a lovely day in Wonderland. Alice was walking in the woods when she spotted the White Rabbit, who was in a great hurry.

"Is everything all right?" she asked.

The White Rabbit stopped. "The Queen of Hearts is hungry, but nothing in the palace seems to satisfy her.

If I don't find her a tasty treat soon, she'll have my head!"

"Perhaps I can help," Alice said. "I never had any trouble finding something to eat in Wonderland. If we work together, I'm sure we will find something that makes the Queen happy."

The White Rabbit sighed. "I do hope you are right!" he said.

"Have you tried asking the Mad Hatter?" Alice asked. "His tea table is always filled with treats."

"Oh, no. I try to steer clear of the hatter," the White Rabbit replied. "He's always causing trouble."

"That's true," Alice said. "But it's still worth a try."

Alice started down the path to the Mad Hatter's house. Suddenly, she stopped short. "Perhaps we don't have to visit the Mad Hatter after all," she said, studying a bush. "Look at these cupcakes! Don't they look tasty?"

Alice plucked a
cupcake from the
bush, and she
and the White
Rabbit hurried
to the palace.

"There you
are!" the Queen
of Hearts yelled when
she spied the rabbit. Then
she saw Alice. "You!" she shouted. "Off with your—"

Alice didn't give the Queen a chance to finish. "We brought you a
cupcake, Your Majesty," she said, handing the Queen the treat.

The Queen actually smiled. "Why, thank you," she said, reaching for it.

Before the Queen could take a bite, the cupcake began to move. Two
wings opened up, and it flew away. It wasn't a cupcake at all. It was a bird!

Alice and the White Rabbit quickly ran from the palace. They hadn't
gone far when the Cheshire Cat appeared on the path in front of them.

"We need to find a snack for the Queen," Alice told him.

The Cheshire Cat looked down at the berries on the bush beneath him.
"Take her some of these blue berries," he suggested.

"But these aren't blueberries," Alice said. "They're red!"

"Red or blue, they're quite tasty," the Cheshire Cat said.

"The Queen is very impatient," the White Rabbit said. "And we don't have anything else to bring her. . . ."

Alice agreed. It seemed they had no choice. She and the White Rabbit picked the berries and took them to the Queen. She promptly gobbled them down.

"Delicious!" she cried. "I suppose you may keep your heads after all!"

Alice and the White Rabbit breathed a sigh of relief. They were so happy they had found something to satisfy the Queen. They started to back down the stairs.

But then the Queen noticed something: her fingers were blue! So were
her hands, and her arms . . .

"What have you done?" she shrieked.

"Oh, dear," Alice said. "That must be why the Cheshire Cat called them
blue berries. They look red, but they turn you
blue when you eat them!"

"Fix me!" the
Queen yelled.

The White
Rabbit nervously
tapped his
paws together.
"Whatever will we
do?"

"I have an
idea," Alice said.

She ran back to the bush where they had seen the Cheshire Cat. Next to it was a bush with blue berries. She quickly picked some and then hurried back to the Queen.

"Eat these!" Alice urged her.

The Queen scowled. "Why should I trust you?"

"Well, I'm just guessing," Alice replied, "but if you don't try, you'll stay blue."

The Queen frowned and ate some of the blue berries. Slowly, the blue faded from her skin.

"I suppose that worked," the Queen said. "But I'm still hungry!"

Alice and the White Rabbit hurried off to find another snack for the Queen. Soon they bumped into Tweedledum and Tweedledee. The twins were dancing and singing a silly song.

Alice noticed that each one was clutching two handfuls of yummy-looking lollipops.

"Excuse me," she said. "We just happen to be looking for a tasty treat for the Queen. May we have a lollipop?"

"If it's for the Queen, we can't say no," said Tweedledum.

"So take a lollipop and go!" finished Tweedledee, handing Alice a bright red lollipop.

Alice and the White Rabbit quickly took the red lollipop to the Queen of Hearts.

"Hmmm," said the Queen. "I do like lollipops. Let me give it a try."

She licked the lollipop and smiled. Then her face turned bright red with heat.

"Spicy! Spicy!" she yelled. "Somebody bring me some water!"

While the guards rushed to help the Queen, Alice and the White Rabbit slipped away from the palace again.

"That's it, I'm going to the Mad Hatter's house," Alice said. "I'm sure he will have a good snack for the Queen."

"I'll wait here," the White Rabbit said.

Alice quickly made her way to the Mad Hatter's house. She found him serving tea to the March Hare.

"Excuse me," she said, "but I was wondering if you could help. The White Rabbit and I need to bring the Queen of Hearts a snack in a hurry. She's very hungry."

The March Hare's ears perked up. "The Queen, you say?" He looked at the Mad Hatter.

"Yes, I did," Alice replied.

The Mad Hatter grinned. He handed a cookie to Alice.

"This is exactly what she needs," he promised.

So Alice and the White Rabbit took the cookie to the Queen of Hearts. She sniffed it.

"It smells good," she said, frowning suspiciously. "And it looks tasty."

The Queen bit into the cookie. "It *is* tasty," she said.

Suddenly, something very strange happened. The Queen began to shrink! She got smaller and smaller until she was no bigger than the cookie. The Queen looked around her throne and realized what was happening. She became very angry and started shouting at Alice and the White Rabbit.

"Guards! Guards! Off with their heads!" she yelled.

But her voice was so tiny and squeaky that the guards didn't hear her.

Alice and the White Rabbit hurried away.

"The Mad Hatter was right," Alice said with a giggle. "That cookie *is* what the Queen needed!"

Fire Pup
of the Day

One morning at their farm, Rolly watched the start of a new day from his favorite sunny spot.

His father, Pongo, accompanied Roger to milk the cows. His mother, Perdita, watched Anita collect eggs. Their housekeeper, Nanny, picked fresh apples from a tree.

If Nanny was picking apples, it could mean only one thing: she planned to bake an apple pie that afternoon! Rolly yipped with glee. He ran inside to tell the others.

He found his siblings watching *The Thunderbolt Adventure Hour* on TV. The canine hero was putting out a fire.

"Go, Thunderbolt, go!" Penny yelled.

"Penny! Patch!" Rolly shouted. "I have good news!" But his siblings weren't listening.

"One day, I'll be a fire hero just like Thunderbolt!" Patch exclaimed.

"Me too!" Penny replied.

"Oh, yeah?" Patch asked. "You think you're fast enough?"

"Sure am!" Penny yelled. "Race ya!"

Rolly sighed as his siblings sprinted toward the front door—just as
Roger, Anita, and Nanny came inside.

"Whoa there, Patch!" Roger cried as milk sloshed on the pup.

"Careful, Penny!" Anita exclaimed as an egg splattered near their feet.

"Oh, boy," Nanny added, laughing. "Our house has gone to the dogs!"

Pongo and Perdita were right behind them.

"Settle down, children," Pongo said. "You must be more careful."

"But, Dad," Penny pleaded, "we're practicing to become fire pups!"

"I see," Perdita replied. "I have an idea! Let's go to the barn."

In the barn, Perdita and Pongo set up a series of challenges.

"Now, puppies," Perdita said, "we'll have three fire safety training exercises to see if any of you are ready to become junior fire pups!"

The puppies barked their approval.

"Firefighters must keep their hoses neat," Perdita explained. "Let's see

how quickly you can coil a garden hose."

Patch, Penny, and Rolly ran in circles with their hoses.

Rolly tried his best, but when he finished, he had tangled himself into one giant knot!

Patch and Penny laughed. They had coiled their hoses perfectly.

"Firefighters use ladders to rescue people," Perdita said. "Let's see who can climb the ladder fastest!"

The puppies hurried up the ladder. But Rolly was afraid of heights. He became dizzy and fell, bumping each rung on the way down. *Clunk, clunk, clunk!*

Perdita rushed to him. "Oh, no, Rolly! Are you hurt?"

"I'm fine," Rolly said. He was just disappointed.

The final challenge was to run to the fire hydrant at the farm's edge.

"What's the use?" Rolly sighed. "I can barely keep up."

"You're doing wonderfully," Perdita told him. "Don't give up."

"We're all different, and that's what makes us special," said Pongo. Rolly shrugged. He didn't feel special.

Rolly reluctantly went
to the starting line.
"Ready . . . set . . . go!"
Perdita yelled. Penny
and Patch raced off
across the farm.
They were neck
and neck in the race.

Rolly quickly fell
behind. He knew he
would never catch up with
his brother and sister. Rolly felt sad that
he didn't have what it took to be a fire pup. Disheartened, he stopped to
catch his breath in front of the kitchen window. But he noticed something
unusual. He'd expected to smell Nanny's delicious apple pie, but instead he
smelled smoke!

Rolly forgot about the race and scuttled inside to the kitchen.

Sure enough, smoke rose from the oven. The pie was burning!

Rolly thought about what Thunderbolt would do. He gathered all his might and barked as loud as he could.

Soon Anita, Roger, and Nanny ran in.

"Oh, my!" Nanny exclaimed. "I forgot about my pie!"

She switched off the oven while Anita and Roger opened the windows. Pongo, Perdita, and Patch arrived to see all the smoke.

"Good thing you came along, Rolly," Roger said. "Otherwise there could have been a real fire!"

"You're a hero!" Anita exclaimed.

"Say," said Roger, "why don't we stop by the firehouse so we can tell the team about our very own fire pup?"

Rolly smiled as Anita and Nanny agreed.

Nanny gave the puppies some pie scraps.

"See, Rolly?" Pongo said. "Like I told you earlier, our differences make us special."

"I guess it's not always important to be the fastest," Patch admitted.

"Or the strongest," Penny added.

"But we can all be brave and save the day!" Rolly said with his mouth full.

Even though Nanny's pie was burned, it still tasted great to Rolly. He was very proud of himself for a job well done. He started to believe that maybe he could be just as brave as Thunderbolt!

The trip to the firehouse was everything Rolly had dreamed it would be!

He saw fire trucks, met real firefighters, and even tried on a fire helmet.

"Great work today, Rolly," the captain said. "You must have a real nose for fire safety!"

Everyone laughed.

I could get used to being a hero, Rolly thought with a smile.

A Wild Night Out

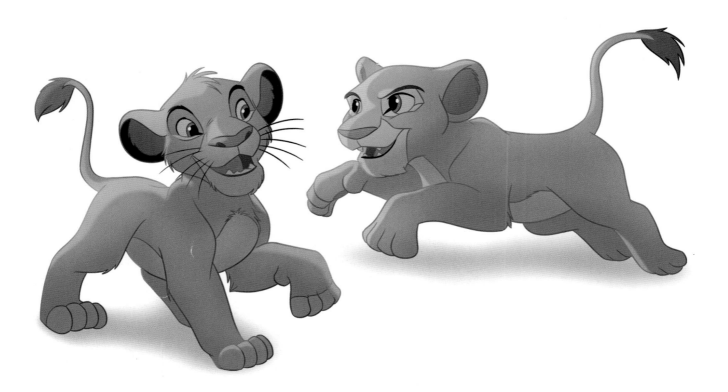

I t was late at night in the Pride Lands. In their den, the lions were all fast asleep. All, that is, except for Simba. Simba just wasn't tired!

Suddenly, the little prince heard a noise coming from outside. Simba perked up his ears and listened harder. *Scratch-scratch.* There it was again—a strange scratching, snuffling sound.

Simba carefully moved away from his mother and padded over to where Nala was sleeping. "Nala! Wake up!" he whispered.

"Hmm?" Nala yawned. Her eyes fluttered open slightly before closing again. "Oh, it's you, Simba," she groaned. "Go back to sleep. I was having the nicest dream. . . ."

"But there's something outside!" Simba said. "Come on! Don't you want to find out what it is?"

Nala opened her eyes again, this time more slowly. "Right now? But it's so dark!"

"So?" Simba replied, grinning. "You're not *scared*, are you?"

"Who? Me?" Nala sprang up like a grasshopper. "Of course I'm not scared!" she told Simba. "Let's go."

Together, Simba and Nala tiptoed past their mothers and the rest of the sleeping pride. They paused at the edge of the den and peered out into the night.

Scratch-scratch.

"What was that?" Nala asked.

"I told you. There's something out there!" Simba said. He squinted his eyes. "See anything?"

Nala shook her head. "Nope. Do you?"

Simba poked his head out a little farther. "Nothing," he said. He was just pulling his head back into the den when a big clump of dirt landed right in the middle of his face!

"Look! Over there!" Nala said as Simba pawed the dirt off his nose.

Simba followed her gaze, his bright eyes growing round.

A shadowy figure shuffled out from behind a tall mound of dirt. The creature looked like it had two tails, one in the front of its body and one in the back.

"What is it?" Nala asked.

Simba shrugged. Whatever it was, it was the strangest-looking animal he had ever seen!

Simba wasn't about to let
this mystery go unsolved.
"Hello!" he called. "Hey!
You! Over here!"

Startled, the creature
looked up.

"Are you lost?" Nala
asked. "Why aren't you
home in bed sleeping?"

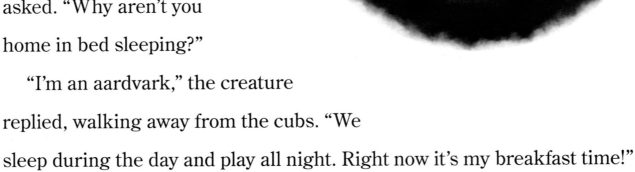

"I'm an aardvark," the creature
replied, walking away from the cubs. "We
sleep during the day and play all night. Right now it's my breakfast time!"

"I wish *we* could sleep all day and play all night," Simba said. He looked
up at the branch of a nearby tree, where the bossy hornbill Zazu was
perched, fast asleep. "Then there would be no Zazu awake to spy on us all
day long and tell us what to do!"

Simba and Nala hurried after the aardvark, who had started digging. The cubs watched, wide-eyed, as the aardvark stuck his gooey tongue into the hole he'd made in the side of a large mound.

When he pulled it out, they could see that his tongue was even longer than Simba's tail—and completely covered with fat, squirmy termites!

When the aardvark had eaten his fill of bugs, he turned away and started to waddle off into the night.

"Wait!" Simba called. "Where are you going?"

"To find my friends," the aardvark said. "Do you want to come?"

Simba and Nala knew a good invitation when they heard one. Without another thought, they bounded after the aardvark.

The cubs hadn't gone far when Simba stepped on something sharp. "Ouch!" he cried, looking at his foot. A little needle was sticking out of it.

Nala peered around. "Look," she said. "They're everywhere. What are they?"

"Sorry," someone behind them said. "I can't help it. Sometimes they just fall out by themselves."

Simba and Nala spun around. Behind them was a little creature with lots of sharp needles all over his back.

"What are all those spikes for?" Simba asked.

"Let's just say they keep anyone from bothering me," the porcupine answered with a wink.

Just then, Simba realized that the aardvark had gotten ahead of them. The cubs chased after him and found him talking to a springhare with a long, long tail and short front legs. The springhare suggested a jumping contest, and Nala and Simba accepted right away. They had always thought of themselves as good pouncers. After all, they practiced every day.

"You might want to reconsider," the aardvark said.

Simba laughed, but one jump into the contest, his laughter faded. The springhare had jumped three times as far as the cubs. After two jumps, she had practically disappeared!

Simba and Nala knew when they were beat. Turning around, they walked back over to where the aardvark was happily digging.

"Are you hungry?" the aardvark asked Simba and Nala.

The cubs' stomachs grumbled. They weren't used to being up so late after dinner.

"A little," Simba admitted.

But when Simba and Nala remembered what the aardvark was eating, they decided maybe they weren't quite so hungry after all.

"Do you have anything else to eat?" Simba asked.

"You mean besides termites?" the aardvark asked. He thought for a minute. Then he bounded off a few feet. "Take a look at this," he called back to them.

"What is it?" Nala asked.

"Ants!" the aardvark answered. "Though I usually save those for dessert."

Suddenly, a cold wind ruffled the cubs' fur.

"Did it just get darker?" Simba asked, shivering.

"And colder?" Nala asked.

Nala and Simba both yawned. The night had been quite an adventure, but they were both starting to get tired. The idea of their cozy den was calling them back home.

But as Simba looked around, he realized he didn't have any idea where the den *was*.

"Which way did we come from?" Simba asked.

Nala looked around. "I'm not sure," she said. "It's too dark."

The cubs searched for something familiar—a landmark that might help them find their way home. But nothing looked right in the dark. They couldn't see far enough.

"I guess we'll have to stay here until morning," Simba said with a sigh. He turned to the aardvark. "How long until sunrise?"

"Sunrise?" the aardvark said. "It's not even time for lunch!"

"Wait!" Nala cried suddenly. High above them, the clouds had parted, revealing the moon. Its light shone on the path Simba and Nala had been looking for. In the distance, they could see Pride Rock.

The cubs said goodbye to their new friend and hurried back home.
Tiptoeing into their den, they saw that everyone was still asleep. Happily,
Simba and Nala snuggled in close to their mothers.

"Good night, Simba," Nala purred.

"See you in the morning." Simba paused to yawn. "What's for breakfast,
do you think?"

"Anything sounds good," Nala said, "as long as it's not bugs!"

Peter Pan

An Adventure for Wendy

Peter Pan and the Lost Boys loved listening to Wendy's bedtime stories. Tinker Bell, too, never missed a telling. They all delighted in Wendy's gripping tales of swashbuckling pirates, hidden treasures, and magical pixie dust.

But one night during
story time, the Lost Boys all
looked bored. Even Michael
and John found their sister's
tale dull.

"Please, tell us a new
story," Michael said.

"Where will I find the
inspiration for a fresh
story?" Wendy wondered
aloud. Then it came to her.
Wendy's bedtime stories
all starred Peter Pan. All
she needed for a brand-new
story was an adventure with
Peter.

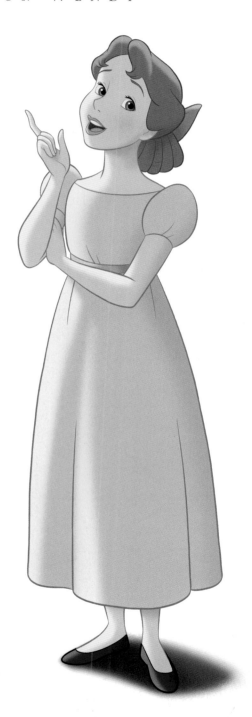

The next morning, Wendy bounded out of bed, ready to join Peter Pan on an exciting excursion. But Peter was nowhere to be found.

"I'm sorry, old chaps," John said to the Lost Boys, pushing up his glasses. "I saw Peter and Tink leaving extra early for their outing this morning."

"You need Peter Pan to have an adventure," declared Nibs.

"What will you do, Wendy?" asked Tootles.

It was true. Peter was always the daring hero of Wendy's stories. But Wendy wasn't concerned. "Now, boys, don't you worry," said Wendy. "I'll just have to create my own adventure."

The Lost Boys looked doubtful. But Wendy was determined. "I'll head for the sea," she said. "There's always adventure to be had there."

Wendy took
a shortcut
through the
jungle on
her way to
the water. She
ran under the
rushing waterfall,
skipped over the
stepping stones, and
greeted the hippopotamus
that lived in the river.

Then she looked up to see
an orangutan family racing between
the trees. "That looks like a grand time!" exclaimed Wendy. "Finding an
adventure can wait a little while longer, I'm sure."

So Wendy joined the fun up above. She and the orangutans swung high above the ground, from tree to tree to tree.

"I wish I could spend all day with you," said Wendy when everyone stopped to rest. "But I'm in search of an adventure." She would not let the Lost Boys down.

Wendy said goodbye to her new friends, then headed toward the bluffs that met the sea.

As Wendy skipped past the shimmering Mermaid
Lagoon, she heard someone cry out, "Help!"

"Oh, dear!" gasped Wendy. A mermaid was stuck in a fishing net. Her friends were nowhere to be seen. Finding a bedtime story would have to wait once again. Wendy dove into the water, swam toward the mermaid, and rescued her from the net.

"Thank you for saving me," gushed the mermaid. "You're so brave. Won't you stay and play in the lagoon for a while?"

Wendy and the mermaid splashed and laughed in the water. "This is so much fun!" cried Wendy as she came up from a dip in the cove. "But I really must be going. I still have to find my adventure."

She left her mermaid friend and went off in search of her bedtime story.

Wendy hiked along
the coast, past Blind
Man's Bluff, heading
toward the Lost Boys'
rowboat moored at
the dock. Once she
reached the boat,
Wendy thought, she
could finally start
her adventure. Then
she'd have a bedtime
story to tell.

But when Wendy arrived at
the rowboat, she found Smee trying to steal it.

Her bedtime story would have to wait. She couldn't let Smee take the
Lost Boys' boat!

"Now, Smee, you leave that boat alone," warned Wendy. "It belongs to the Lost Boys."

The pirate grinned. "You'll have to fight me for it first, little lass," he challenged.

Wendy dueled with Smee, using all the sword skills she'd learned from Peter, and a few tricks of her own. Soon victory was hers, as was the boat.

Her adventure could finally begin.

But as Wendy looked to the sky, she saw the sun was setting on the horizon. It was time to head back.

Wendy returned to the hideout feeling defeated. She'd failed to have an adventure. There would be no new bedtime story that night.

She stood outside the hideout, knowing her friends would be disappointed listening to the same old bedtime story. *There's always tomorrow,* she thought as she climbed into the hideout.

When the Lost Boys gathered around, Wendy apologized. "I'm sorry, boys.
I meant to have a marvelous adventure today, but instead I swung through
the trees with the orangutans, saved a mermaid, and fought off a pirate."

The Lost Boys listened in awe. Peter Pan was enthralled. Swinging from
the trees? Swimming in the lagoon? Dueling with Smee?

"Wendy, what a thrilling day you had!" Peter exclaimed.

"You're so courageous," said John.

The Lost Boys all agreed it was the best bedtime story they'd ever heard. "Hooray for Wendy!" they cheered.

Looking back on her day, Wendy realized they were right. She'd created her own adventure all by herself. What a wonderful feeling!

That night, Wendy snuggled into her warm bed, dreaming about all the big adventures she'd have the next day.

Lady and the TRAMP

A Trusty Babysitter

I t was a beautiful evening. Lady and Tramp were dressed up for dinner. It was their anniversary, and Tramp had made reservations at Tony's. He had booked the same table where they had dined on their very first date.

"Come on, Pidge," Tramp called. "We're going to be late."

Lady was busy making sure their puppies—Scooter, Fluffy, Ruffy, and Scamp—were fed, bathed, and ready to be tucked into bed. "Now, be good for your babysitter," she said.

"We will, Mama," the puppies replied.

"You too, Scamp," Tramp said, eyeing his son.

Just then, a knock sounded at the dog door.

"Uncle Trusty!" barked the puppies. Wagging their tails, they pounced on him affectionately and licked his floor-sweeping ears.

"*You're* our babysitter?" Scamp asked.

"I am, indeed," Trusty replied.

"Don't let him give you any trouble," Tramp said.

"Trouble? Why, this little young'un wouldn't dream of giving Uncle Trusty any *trouble*," said the old dog. "Would you, Scamp?"

Lady and Tramp kissed their puppies good night and headed toward the dog door.

"Don't let the puppies stay up too late," Lady told her old friend. "One bedtime story and then it's straight to bed."

"Oh, don't you worry, Miss Lady," Trusty said. "If my grandpappy taught me anything, it's how to put a dog to bed! I'll have 'em snoring away like an old sawmill in no time."

Trusty followed the puppies to the parlor and settled on a cozy cushion right next to their bed. "Now then . . . where was I . . . ?" he said.

"You were going to tell us a bedtime story," Scooter said.

"Oh, yes!" Trusty chuckled. "A bedtime story! Fine idea! Don't mind if I do! Let's see now. . . . How does it begin . . . ? Once upon a . . ."

"Time?" Fluffy suggested.

"No . . ." Uncle Trusty shook his head. "Or, wait. Maybe yes! That sounds familiar. Once upon a time . . ." he restarted. "Er . . . eh . . . where was I again?"

While Trusty tried to remember his story, Scooter, Fluffy, and Ruffy yawned and closed their eyes. Soon they were fast asleep.

Trusty smiled down at the pups. "Well, now, that wasn't so hard," he said. "I don't know why Lady went on so. I do declare, there's nothin' to puttin' pups to bed! Sweet dreams, little young'uns."

Trusty leaned over the puppies' basket to give each one a gentle peck. "Wait one doggone minute," he said as he came to the third and final furry forehead. "Weren't there four of you before . . . ?"

Scamp was gone!

"Which way did he go?" Trusty asked, turning around. He turned two more times, but Scamp still wasn't there.

Trusty put his nose to the floor in search of Scamp's trail.

Unfortunately, Trusty's sense of smell had been gone for years. But that
had never stopped him before, and it wasn't going to now!

Trusty sniffed and sniffed, following his nose . . . straight into the piano!
"Oh, excuse me, ma'am," he said.

Slowly, Trusty made his way to the kitchen, which looked as if a storm had just blown through it. There were smashed eggs everywhere. Milk bottles lay empty, their contents forming puddles on the floor. Big sacks of flour had been torn apart!

"I'd say the pup's been here," Trusty said with a sigh.

Scamp wasn't there anymore, but he had left behind a trail of floury paw prints.

Trusty followed the prints into the living room. It looked even worse than the kitchen. Jim Dear's newspaper was in tatters, and his slippers were torn to shreds. Darling's knitting had been unraveled. Yarn crisscrossed the room like a giant spiderweb.

"Which way did he go?" Trusty said again. He followed the yarn around and around and around the room, until at last it led him back into the hall and to the doggy door.

"Scamp?" Trusty called, eyeing the holes dug all over the yard. "Scamp, you come on back in here, you hear me? Listen to Uncle Trusty, now."

But if Scamp heard Trusty, he wasn't letting on.

Trusty was about to call Scamp again when he noticed a hole at the base of the wooden fence. His old heart began to thump loudly.

Trusty hurried over to the fence as fast as his stiff old legs would allow. "Doggone it! The pup's gone and flown the coop!" he moaned. What was he going to do?

Trusty poked his head
through the hole and then
quickly pulled it back. He
had seen Lady and Tramp
strolling down the street
toward home.

Poor Trusty! His beloved
Lady had left her dear little
puppies in his care and
protection, and he had let her
son run away.

Trusty plodded back
into the house and sat by
the doggy door to meet the
couple and break the bad
news to them.

"Trusty!" Tramp said, beaming, as he and Lady stepped through the door. "How did it go?"

Before Trusty could answer, Lady pranced up and kissed his cheek. "Dear Trusty. We really can't thank you enough. Let us go peek in on the puppies, shall we? Then you can tell us how everything went!"

Trusty hung his head and followed Lady into the parlor, dreading the story he had to tell. How was he going to explain that he had lost Scamp?

Suddenly, Lady turned around. "Trusty!" she said. "However did you do this?"

"Er, do what?" he said, confused.

Lady pointed to the puppies' basket. "Why, get Scamp to go to bed, of course. Even we have trouble making him settle down."

"Well, would you look at that," Tramp said, eyeing his son. "Well done, old chap. I'll tell you something: we'll definitely be asking you to babysit again!"

Disney
DUMBO

Timothy's Big Day

TIMOTHY
MOUSE

CIRCUS

Timothy Q. Mouse looked out over the edge of Dumbo's hat and grinned. Below him, the crowd cheered for the flying elephant.

Timothy loved the circus. There was no place in the world he would rather be.

Later that night, Timothy watched the crew pack up the circus. It was time to move on to the next town. But first the Ringmaster had to pass out letters and packages to the performers.

Unseen by the Ringmaster, a tiny envelope fell out of his pile.

Timothy scurried over to the fallen letter. The mouse turned the envelope over to see who it was for and then gasped. It was for him!

Timothy couldn't believe it. His family was coming to see him! He hadn't

spoken to them since he'd left home to join the circus. To his parents, life

on the farm was perfect. They couldn't imagine living anywhere else.

Timothy hurried over to Dumbo's stall.

"Oh, boy. Look at this, will ya?" Timothy shouted, waving around the letter. "My parents are coming to see you perform, Dumbo. They've never liked the circus, but seeing our show will change that! After all, who wouldn't love a flying elephant?"

As the circus traveled to his hometown, Timothy grew more and more excited about seeing his family.

But Timothy was nervous, too. What if his parents didn't think he'd done a good job with Dumbo after all? He wanted them to be proud of him. And that meant he *had* to show them how great circus life was.

The next morning, the circus train pulled into the station. After so long away, Timothy felt strange to know that he was home again.

He wondered if he would see his family in the crowd. But there were too many people. If the mice had come, there was no way he'd be able to find them.

Finally, the animals arrived at the circus site. Timothy watched as the circus hands got to work setting up the big top. No matter how many times he saw it, watching the tent go up never got any less exciting.

"Just wait until my family gets a load of this," Timothy said to Dumbo. "The lights. The noise. And you, Dumbo. I can't wait for them to see your act."

But at that moment, Dumbo let out a great big sneeze.

Dumbo sneezed again. And again.

"Oh, no," the Ringmaster said, hurrying over to look at the little elephant. "This is no good. You can't go on with a cold, and we can't go on without you."

The Ringmaster turned to the circus hands. "Sorry, lads. This fella needs his rest. Today's show will have to wait."

Timothy looked over at Dumbo. The Ringmaster was right: the little elephant did not look good at all.

"It's my job to take care of you, Dumbo," Timothy said with determination. "Let's find you somewhere comfortable to lie down."

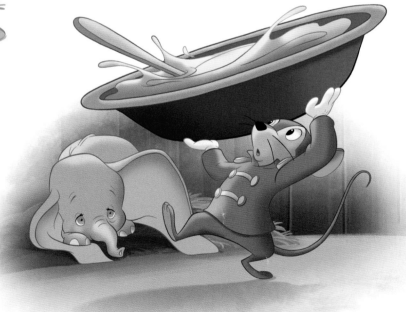

Timothy led Dumbo to a cozy pile of hay and went to get a steaming bowl of peanut soup.

Then Timothy started to give Dumbo a warm bath, but Dumbo sneezed again.

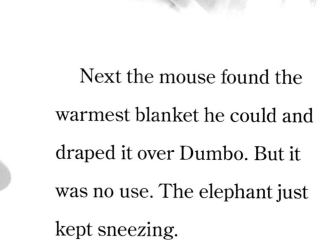

Next the mouse found the warmest blanket he could and draped it over Dumbo. But it was no use. The elephant just kept sneezing.

"Well, the least I can do is make sure you get some peace and quiet so you can rest," Timothy said, moving to the front of the tent.

He felt bad for Dumbo. It was no fun to be sick. But he felt bad for himself, too. This was supposed to be his chance to make his parents proud of him.

Timothy was still feeling sorry
for himself a few hours later
when he heard a familiar
voice. "Timothy, dear.
We have been looking
for you everywhere!"

Timothy turned
to see his mother,
his father, and his
brothers and sisters
standing in front
of him.

"Mother. Father. You're
here." The little mouse hung his head. "I'm afraid
Dumbo has a cold. He can't go on tonight. I'm
sorry you wasted your time coming."

"Wasted our time?" Timothy's father asked. "We came to the circus to see *you*. We're not big-city travelers, but we're certainly not going to miss a chance to see our son!"

"You don't think I made a mistake joining the circus?" Timothy asked.

"There's no such thing as a mistake as long as you're doing what you love," his mother said.

At that moment, the flaps to Dumbo's tent rustled, and the little elephant stepped through, looking like he felt much better.

"Dumbo, old pal," Timothy said, "may I introduce you to my family?"

Dumbo was very pleased to meet them.

"If you'll excuse me," Timothy said to everyone, "I'd better let the Ringmaster know that Dumbo is feeling better." Then he turned to his parents. "Wait here, you two. I have something I'd like to show you."

That night, Timothy sat in his usual spot in Dumbo's hat—with his parents next to him! Cheers filled the room as the elephant soared through the air.

"All those happy faces are pretty special," Timothy's father said. "Maybe I'm starting to understand this circus thing after all."

Timothy's mother nodded. "Tell me," she said, "can this elephant go any faster?"

Ride the Waves

It was a hot, lazy afternoon on the island of Kauai. Lilo and Stitch were at their favorite place: the beach. Lilo took pictures. And Stitch— well, Stitch did what he did best. He caused mischief!

Lilo's older sister, Nani, was also at the beach with David. When they noticed Stitch was getting into trouble, they rushed right over.

"Guys, you can't just dash all over the beach causing trouble!" said Nani when things were calm again.

"How about you two put your energy to good use?" said David. "The Kauai Kurl Surf Competition is next Saturday. Nani and I are entering. You should, too!"

A surfing competition? No way. That was Nani's thing, not Lilo's. Lilo loved the beach and liked to swim, but getting on a surfboard without her sister made her nervous.

"I don't think so," said Lilo, shaking her head.

Beside her, Stitch shook his own head so fast he almost fell backward!

"Come on," said Nani. "I'll teach you both how to surf like champions!"

Lilo hadn't thought of it that way. If surfing meant more time with Nani and Stitch . . . Lilo would do it for *'ohana*, the family!

"Okay, we're in!" said Lilo, and everyone high-fived.

First stop: the surf shop!

"We have to rent you a board," said Nani as they walked into the store. She studied the wall of colorful surfboards. They towered over Lilo and Stitch.

Stitch was mesmerized by all the boards. He loved every single one! Nani looked for the perfect board for two little surfers.

"Hey, Lilo," said Myrtle, a classmate. Lilo and Myrtle didn't always get along. "I didn't know you were a surfer."

"I didn't know you were a surfer, either," said Lilo. "Anyway, my sister, Nani, is going to help me surf like a champion for the competition next weekend."

"I've entered the competition, too . . . and *I'm* going to win!" said Myrtle.

"Don't worry, Lilo," said Nani as they left the surf shop. "Surfing isn't about winning. It's about having fun, right?"

Lilo wasn't so sure. She was beginning to wonder why she had agreed to enter the competition in the first place. Oh, right . . . for *'ohana*.

Lilo felt better once Myrtle was gone and she was back on the beach. Stitch ran straight for the ocean, but Nani stopped him. She had Stitch and Lilo place the board on the sand.

"You are going to have to get out on the waves all by yourself," Nani said. "First lie down flat on your belly.

"Now paddle with your arms. Imagine a big wave is coming, and push up quickly. Plant both feet on the board at the same time, and . . . there! That was good, Lilo!"

Maybe I can do this, Lilo thought.

"You're supposed to do that in the water, I think," boomed a big voice, followed by some laughter. It was their friend Mr. Bubbles!

"Nani is teaching us in the sand first," said Lilo. "But I think we're ready to try it out there!" Lilo pointed to the waves, and Stitch nodded.

"Okay, then," said Nani, smiling. "Remember, if you get knocked down, just get right back up again."

Lilo and Stitch picked up the surfboard and headed for the water.

Lilo and Stitch paddled out. Nani followed on her own board. The whole family was together on the ocean!

For the rest of the week, Lilo and Stitch focused on strength training and practicing their surfing technique.

By Friday, Lilo and Stitch were riding the waves! Lilo's body felt strong and steady.

Finally, it was the big day.

"I'm nervous," Lilo said.

"Lilo, you've been practicing all week," Nani replied, "and your hard work will pay off. Just do your best. I'll be right out there with you. . . . We'll show the competition what the Pelekai sisters can do!"

"And Stitch?" said Stitch.

"Yes, of course!" said Nani. "Stitch, too! Let's go!"

At the beach, they saw many of the competitors lined up with their surfboards, their eyes fixed on the waves.

Lilo joined them. She was focused. She was tough. She was—

"Intimidated?" said Myrtle, interrupting Lilo's thoughts. "You should be. Get ready to wave goodbye to first place!"

But Lilo didn't let Myrtle get to her. Instead, she remembered what Nani had said. She had practiced. She was ready.

The official blew the whistle. Everyone
ran to the water. Together, Lilo and
Stitch paddled out, jumped up,
and stuck the landing with all
four of their feet.

"Go, Lilo and Stitch! Go!"
shouted Nani and David across
the waves.

Myrtle hit a wave the wrong way and totally wiped
out. Instead of getting back on her board, Myrtle
dragged herself to shore.

Lilo and Stitch were riding high! It felt great to be out on the ocean, their faces against the wind, surfing so well. Lilo glanced at the judges on the beach. *We'll show them what we can do,* she thought.

"Should we try out a trick, Stitch?" Lilo asked.

Stitch nodded, an excited grin on his face. He bit the board leash. Lilo swung him around and around and around, and . . .

Oh, no! Wipeout!

Fortunately, Nani was
close by. She came to the rescue.

"Lilo, Stitch! Are you okay?" asked Nani as she pulled them onto her board.

Lilo coughed up some seawater. "I think so, but our board is gone. We'll never win now!" she moaned.

Nani smiled. "The most important thing isn't winning, right? It's—"

"Getting right back up again when you get knocked down?" finished Lilo.

"Yes. Now let's show them what we can do . . . together!" said Nani.

Soon a massive wave came. "Imagine your heart and the wave's heart are one and the same," Nani said. The words helped Lilo feel braver.

Lilo hopped up onto Nani's shoulders, and Stitch scrambled onto Lilo's shoulders. Together, they surfed all the way to shore.

Lilo, Stitch, and Nani won the award for best teamwork. The whole family—*'ohana*—did it together!

The special prize was a trophy and a new surfboard.

"For me?" Lilo asked.

"For you, Lilo," said Nani. "You deserve it. And now we can keep practicing . . . for next year's surfing competition!"

Disney
Robin hood
Castle Rescue

Robin Hood whistled as he stirred a pot of soup. The hero was hidden deep in Sherwood Forest. His job was tricky lately. Prince John and the Sheriff of Nottingham were trying their best to capture him.

Luckily, Robin Hood had good friends on his side. Little John, Friar Tuck, and Maid Marian were all helping him come up with plans to help the people of Nottingham.

"Don't burn the soup, Rob!" Little John called as he and Maid Marian arrived with wood for the fire.

"I'll only make that mistake once," Robin Hood answered, handing out soup to his friends.

Robin was about to take a sip when Friar Tuck appeared! The friar was out of breath and looked very worried.

"Friar Tuck! Is something wrong?" Maid Marian asked.

"Skippy is missing!" Friar Tuck said. He explained that Skippy, the young rabbit, had lost an arrow in Prince John's castle and gone in looking for it. His friend Toby had waited a long time for him to come back, but Skippy had never returned.

"He must be lost in the castle," Maid Marian said.

"Or worse, Prince John has caught him," Robin said. "I have to rescue Skippy." The fox grabbed his bow and arrows and headed toward the castle.

"I'm coming with you," Maid Marian said.

Robin Hood tried to tell Maid Marian that it was too dangerous, but Marian wouldn't take no for an answer. "I lived in the castle for years," she said. "I know it better than anyone. I'm your best chance to find Skippy before Prince John does. Plus, I know a secret passageway into the castle."

Maid Marian opened the passageway. Robin was impressed. Little John was concerned, but he trusted her. Together, the three friends made their way through it.

With Little John in tow, Robin Hood and Maid Marian soon made it inside the castle. They snuck up and down winding hallways, searching for Skippy at every turn.

Just as they were about to turn another corner, Robin Hood pulled Maid Marian back. He could hear voices coming toward them!

"Quick! We have to turn around!" Robin Hood said. But it was too late. There were voices coming from behind them, too. They were trapped!

Luckily, Robin had an idea. He tied a rope to a notch in the wall. Then he tied the other end to an arrow and fired it out a nearby window—and into another window on the castle's opposite wall.

Robin gave the rope a good yank and then motioned for Maid Marian and Little John to follow him.

The Sheriff of Nottingham and two guards turned the corner just as Little John grabbed the rope and leaped out the window.

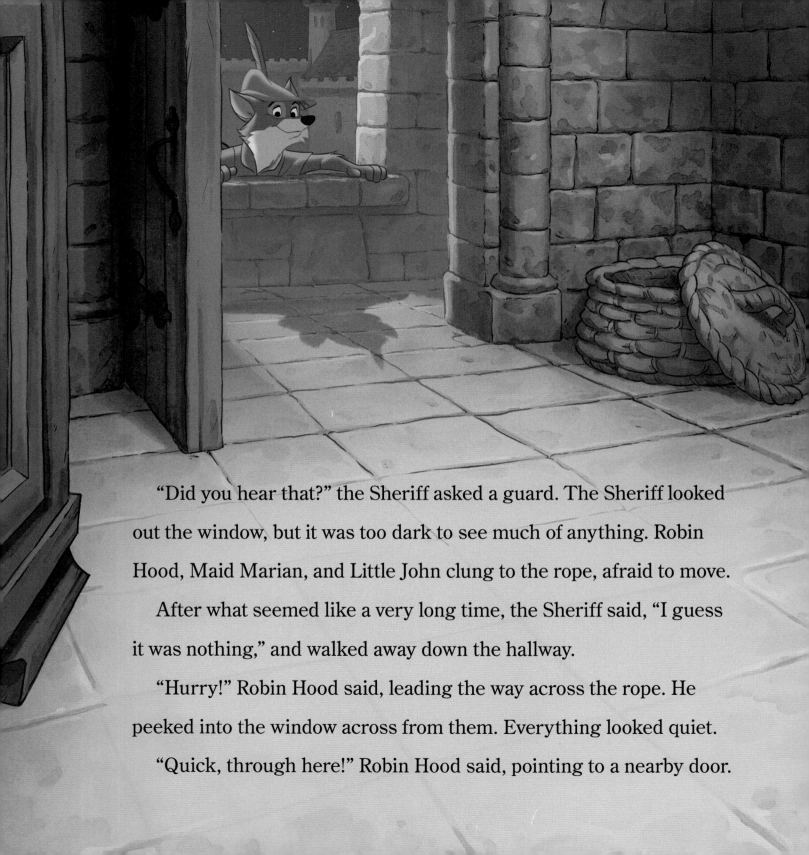

"Did you hear that?" the Sheriff asked a guard. The Sheriff looked out the window, but it was too dark to see much of anything. Robin Hood, Maid Marian, and Little John clung to the rope, afraid to move.

After what seemed like a very long time, the Sheriff said, "I guess it was nothing," and walked away down the hallway.

"Hurry!" Robin Hood said, leading the way across the rope. He peeked into the window across from them. Everything looked quiet.

"Quick, through here!" Robin Hood said, pointing to a nearby door.

"This room looks familiar," Maid Marian said.

But Maid Marian's realization was too late. Robin Hood had already gone through the door—right into Sir Hiss's study. Even worse, Sir Hiss was there!

Maid Marian pointed to a door on the other side of the room. Very slowly, the group crept behind Sir Hiss. Luckily, Sir Hiss was in the middle of doing something very, very important: examining himself in the mirror.

"Sir Hiss, you've outdone yourself with this one!" the snake said to himself as he tried on a new hat.

Robin opened the door and motioned his friends through. They were safe!

Sir Hiss's room opened up into a very large courtyard.

"There!" Little John whispered, pointing to one end of the courtyard. It was Skippy! The rabbit was hiding behind the well.

"Oh, no!" Maid Marian said, pointing at the opposite end of the courtyard. It was Prince John. He was walking right to Skippy's hiding place!

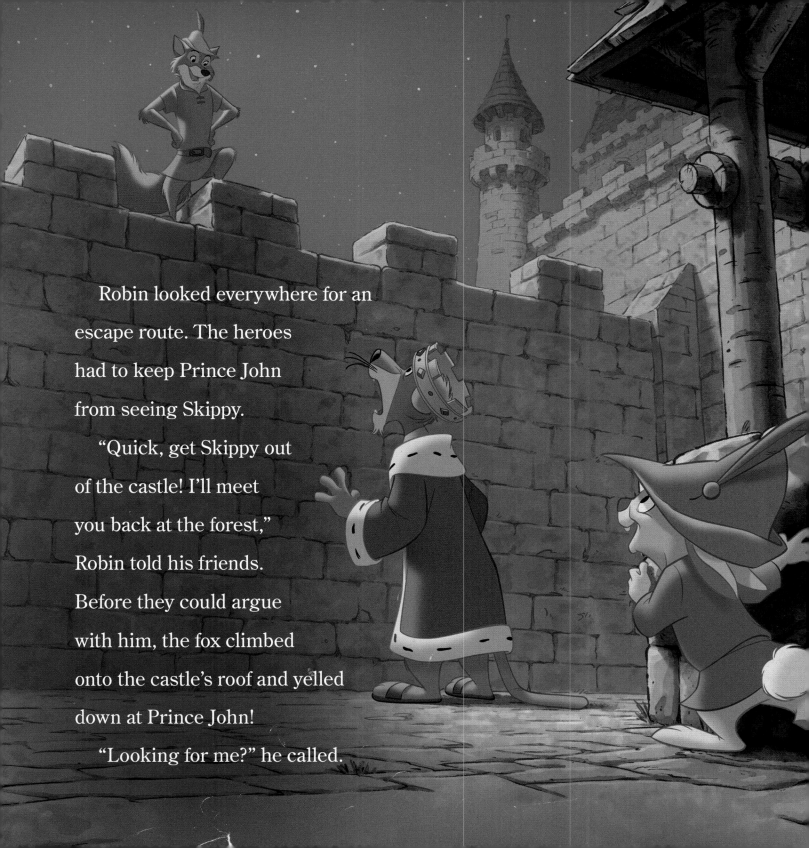

Robin looked everywhere for an escape route. The heroes had to keep Prince John from seeing Skippy.

"Quick, get Skippy out of the castle! I'll meet you back at the forest," Robin told his friends. Before they could argue with him, the fox climbed onto the castle's roof and yelled down at Prince John!

"Looking for me?" he called.

"You! Guards, seize him!" Prince John ordered.

Guards rushed outside and began to shoot arrows at Robin! He ducked behind a chimney, avoiding the arrows just in time.

Prince John was so distracted he didn't notice Little John and Maid Marian in the courtyard. The pair grabbed Skippy and rushed him to the secret passageway.

Seeing that his friends were safe, Robin Hood leaped across the roofs away from Prince John. "Always a pleasure!" he called back over his shoulder.

Back in the forest, Skippy, Maid Marian, and Little John waited for Robin.

"I hope he's okay," Skippy said.

"Of course I am!" Robin said, appearing out of the trees.

"Robin!" Maid Marian said. "We were worried!"

"I'm safe and sound," Robin said. "And I found something in the castle. Try not to lose this again, Skippy!" He handed Skippy the missing arrow.

"Now, who would like some soup?"

Disney
Pinocchio

A Real Boy

The sun was just beginning to rise over Pinocchio's little village. The moment he awoke, Pinocchio leaped out of bed and ran to look at himself in the mirror.

He laughed with joy when he saw his reflection. It hadn't been a dream. The Blue Fairy had made him a real boy!

Pinocchio lost track of the minutes as he stared at his reflection. He might have stood there all day if he hadn't smelled a wonderful scent coming from the kitchen.

As he sniffed the air, Pinocchio felt a strange sensation: his mouth began to water. *Is this what being hungry feels like?* he wondered.

Pinocchio ran to the kitchen. There he saw his father, Geppetto, cooking a huge breakfast. There were eggs and pancakes and bacon and sausages and oatmeal and orange juice and toast and milk and muffins and . . . Pinocchio stopped trying to name everything on the table.

Geppetto grinned. "I wanted to cook you something special for your first breakfast," he said. "So I made everything!"

Pinocchio's stomach rumbled as he looked at all the food.

"Well, come on," Geppetto said. "Dig in!"

Pinocchio sat down and tried a bite of eggs. "It's fluffy!" he said, his mouth full. "And soft. And . . . delicious!" Pinocchio tried a little bit of all the food Geppetto had made. Every bite tasted different from the last.

"This is wonderful," Pinocchio said. "Can we eat all day long?"

"Oh, no," Geppetto laughed. "We'll be much too busy for that. I have so much to show you."

"Can we take the food with us?" Pinocchio asked.

"That's an excellent idea," Geppetto said. "We'll have a picnic!"

Geppetto packed lunch, and he and Pinocchio left to explore the village.

The first thing Pinocchio noticed was how brightly the sun shone. Its dazzling beams felt warm against his skin.

Pinocchio and Geppetto made a game of running in and out of the shadows all the way to the edge of town. When Pinocchio jumped through the last shadow, he felt a strange sensation in his stomach. It was different from hunger. It was—

Hic. Pinocchio's tummy flip-flopped and a strange sound came from his throat.

"What—*hic*—is going—*hic*—on?" Pinocchio asked. He was starting to get scared.

"Don't worry," Geppetto said. "It's just the hiccups."

"Hiccups?" Pinocchio asked. "Will they ever—*hic*—stop?" Geppetto showed Pinocchio how to hold his breath until the hiccups went away.

Pinocchio wasn't sure he liked this new experience. He had been so busy thinking about how much fun being a real boy was, he hadn't stopped to think about all the things that could go wrong.

Pinocchio grew silent as he followed Geppetto. His mind was filled with questions, but he wasn't sure how to ask many of them. At first, the sun's warmth had felt nice. But now Pinocchio was hot and sweaty. His feet hurt. And his stomach felt as empty as it had that morning before breakfast.

Pinocchio finally asked the question he was most concerned about: "Are we there yet?"

Geppetto took Pinocchio's hand. "It's just over this hill. . . ."

The pair climbed higher until they saw a beautiful valley below them.

"Race you to the swimming hole?" Geppetto asked.

Pinocchio nodded and ran off before Geppetto could get ready.

Father and son ran down the hill and collapsed in a happy pile next

to the lake's edge.

"Time for food!" Pinocchio cheered.

Geppetto laughed and began unpacking the picnic basket.

Geppetto and Pinocchio spent the rest of the day at the swimming hole, playing in the water and fishing on the bank.

As they played, Geppetto told Pinocchio stories of the many times he had visited the lake as a young boy. Pinocchio felt much better now that he had eaten and rested. The cool water was refreshing after their long walk from the village. Even when Pinocchio scraped his knee on one of the willow trees, he didn't get upset. He was starting to realize what an exciting place the whole world was.

As the sun began to set, Pinocchio noticed a new feeling. His eyelids felt heavy, as though he could barely keep his eyes open. Then he yawned.

"I'm tired," Pinocchio said, surprised at the realization.

"You've had quite a big day," Geppetto said.

"Are you ready to go home?"

Pinocchio nodded, and Geppetto lifted him onto his shoulders. He carried Pinocchio toward their little house in the village.

Sitting on Geppetto's back, Pinocchio looked up into the night sky. Far above them shone the Wishing Star, twinkling brightly. Pinocchio realized that being a real boy was more complicated than he had imagined.

"Today was fun, Father," Pinocchio said. "But . . . it was hard, too."

Geppetto nodded, thinking about what Pinocchio had said.
"That's what being alive is. It's sunlight and bacon and hiccups
and scraped knees. Some of it will be scary, but I promise I'll be
right there with you."

Geppetto waited for Pinocchio to answer, but all he heard was the sound of soft snoring. Pinocchio was fast asleep! Geppetto laughed quietly. "Enough speeches. It's time to get you to bed."

Geppetto carried Pinocchio as gently as he could to bed. He fluffed each pillow and then drew the blankets close under Pinocchio's chin.

"Good night, my boy," Geppetto said, leaning in to kiss Pinocchio on the forehead. "Today was a dream come true. I cannot wait to share another adventure with you tomorrow."

Bambi

The Light-Up Night

The golden sun dipped behind the trees, bathing the forest in beautiful twilight. It was time for the animals to go to bed.

In the thicket, the little quails scurried one by one into their nest. The mice cuddled together in the thistles. Thumper and the other bunnies splashed each other as they washed up before bed. Bambi smiled as he curled up next to his mother.

One animal wasn't getting ready for bed, though. In the trees, Friend Owl was just beginning to wake up. He slept all through the day while the other animals were awake.

At night, when the moon rose into the sky, so did the wise old owl.

Friend Owl waved hello to his friends.

"Friend Owl! Tell us a bedtime story!" Thumper hollered. He was so excited that his foot went *thump-thump-thump*.

"Remember your manners," his mother said.

"Sorry," Thumper said. "Tell us a story *please*."

"Not tonight," Friend Owl said. "The shooting stars will soon put on a show, and I don't want to miss it!"

Bambi's ears perked up. What was a shooting star? He wasn't sure—but he wanted to find out. And Bambi wasn't the only one.

"I want to see the shooting stars, too!" Thumper cried.

"It's getting dark," Bambi's mother said in a soft voice. "And it's a long way to the meadow."

"I'll look after the young prince and Thumper," Friend Owl offered. "They'll be safe with me."

Friend Owl flew slowly overhead, watching as Bambi and Thumper pranced along beneath him. In the deepening darkness, Bambi and Thumper could hear the song of the crickets.

All of a sudden, Bambi saw a bright spark. "I saw it!" he cried.

Friend Owl smiled kindly at him.

"No, Bambi," he said. "That was a firefly."

"Oh," Bambi said, watching in wonder as, one by one, fireflies lit up the meadow. It was a beautiful sight, but Bambi and Thumper still wanted to see the shooting stars.

The friends waited quietly as the sky grew darker. Soon there was just a thin sliver of moon gleaming overhead.

"That's good!" Friend Owl said approvingly. "A dark night will make the shooting stars easier to see."

Just then, a brilliant flash lit up the entire sky!

"Look!" Thumper shouted. "I saw the first shooting star!"

But before anyone could respond, a rumble of thunder rolled across the meadow. Thumper hadn't seen a shooting star after all. It was a bolt of lightning!

Bambi, Thumper, and Friend Owl scurried back to the forest as raindrops pelted the meadow. Thick clouds billowed across the sky, blocking the moon and stars. The friends huddled under the canopy of trees, waiting for the storm to pass.

Bambi sighed. With so many clouds covering the sky, how would he ever see a shooting star?

"I guess we'd better go home," Bambi said sadly.

Thumper was too disappointed to even thump his foot.

"Now, now, not so fast, little ones," Friend Owl said reassuringly. "Summer storms blow over before you know it. Be patient. The shooting stars are worth the wait!"

After a while, the steady drumming of the rain began to slow. A cool breeze ruffled the leaves—and blew the clouds from the sky.

"Is it over?" Bambi asked. "Can we see shooting stars now?"

"Let's find out," replied Friend Owl.

At the edge of the meadow, Bambi, Thumper, and Friend Owl saw that the fireflies had stopped flashing and the lightning was over. The night sky was clear but still.

Then it happened: a spark of light, high above them. It plunged toward the ground, leaving a shining white streak behind it!

Bambi gasped in surprise. "Was that it?" he asked. "A real shooting star?"

"That's right, young prince!" Friend Owl hooted happily.

Soon another shooting star zoomed overhead, and another, and another! The night sky was full of them!

The three friends watched the sky for hours. Finally, there were no more stars.

"It's time to go home now," Friend Owl said.

"But I want to see more shooting stars!" Thumper whined.

"And you will," Friend Owl promised. "When the time is right."

Back in the thicket, Bambi snuggled close to his mother. As he told her all about the shooting stars, he closed his eyes. Behind his eyelids, he could still see the brilliant streaks of light. It had been the perfect night!

THE ARISTOCATS

The Surprise Party

Early one morning, Thomas O'Malley yawned, stretched, and found three little kittens jumping on his bed. Marie, Berlioz, and Toulouse began to sing cheerily while Duchess presented O'Malley with a dish of cream.

"Happy birthday!" the cats sang out. "Happy birthday to you, dear Abraham DeLacey Giuseppe Casey Thomas O'Malley!"

"Now, children," Duchess began, "who wants to give Thomas his birthday present first?"

"I do, I do!" Toulouse replied. "Follow me, Mr. O'Malley!"

"Yeah," said Berlioz. "Follow him!"

As soon as O'Malley's back was turned, Duchess whispered to Berlioz and Marie: "Come, children! Let's get on with our plans for Thomas's surprise party!"

Toulouse led O'Malley into the sunroom.

"This is where I do my greatest work," Toulouse announced. "And today I'm gonna paint your portrait. Face this way, please, and don't move!"

Squish! Splurt! Splat! Toulouse began squirting paint from various tubes.

O'Malley was so busy watching Toulouse that he didn't see what was happening behind him.

A little while later, Toulouse finished his painting and presented it proudly to O'Malley.

"That's real swell, Toulouse," O'Malley said. "I don't suppose you could teach me how to do that."

"Sure!" Toulouse replied. "I can teach ya!" He smothered a smile. The birthday surprise plans were right on track!

Toulouse showed O'Malley how to mix paints to get different colors.

Then they outlined a picture. Finally, they painted . . . and painted . . . and painted.

"I never had such birthday fun in my life!" O'Malley said when they were finished. "I can't wait to show this to Scat Cat and the band when we jam!"

Just then, Marie and Berlioz walked into the room.

"Our turn, our turn!" Marie said to O'Malley, climbing to her spot atop the piano. "Would you like to hear some scales and arpeggios?"

"We planned a special birthday song just for you!" Berlioz said. "Wanna hear it?"

"Well, sure I do!" O'Malley said.

Berlioz cracked his toes while Marie moved to the other side of the piano and sat up straight. She made sure O'Malley was looking at her—not outside, where the others were setting up his surprise party.

"Okay," Berlioz said at last. "Are you ready?"

"Ready!" O'Malley replied.

Berlioz stretched along the piano keys and played their new song while Marie sang. O'Malley was loving the tempo and couldn't believe they had written him his very own tune.

"You can join us if you want to, Mr. O'Malley," Marie urged.

Soon O'Malley was singing along. "Thank you for the best birthday song I've ever heard!"

As early evening approached, Duchess intercepted O'Malley.

"Do you want to go for a birthday stroll?" she asked.

"Well, sure," O'Malley said. "That old band can wait. There's nothing I'd rather do than go on a birthday walk—er, stroll—with you."

When they reached the end of the garden, Duchess pulled a wrapped gift from behind a rosebush.

"Happy birthday, dear Thomas," she said, presenting it to him.

"A bow tie! Thanks, Duchess," he said. "Between you and those kittens, this has been a terrific birthday!"

"It's not over yet, you know," Duchess told him. "We do have one last surprise for you."

Duchess led O'Malley into the dining room.

"I hope everything is to your liking," Madame said to O'Malley.

Toulouse, Berlioz, and Marie were there with Roquefort, too.

"Happy birthday!" they all called out.

They had prepared all his favorite foods. O'Malley and Duchess even shared a salmon soufflé.

"Say, what a terrific birthday!" O'Malley said. "I do think it's almost time for bed, though, little ones."

"Before we go to bed, can we go look at the stars?" Marie asked.

"Oh, yes," Duchess agreed as they all headed outside. "That's a wonderful idea. And Thomas! I have to confess—the dinner was your second-to-last birthday surprise. . . ."

"Surprise!" yelled Duchess and the kittens.

"Surprise!" hollered Scat Cat and the band.

"Wow!" O'Malley exclaimed. Turning to Duchess and the kittens, he asked, "How did you pull this off? You were with me all day!"

Marie giggled. "Well, sometimes some of us were with you—"

"While others of us were preparing," Duchess concluded.

When the night finally ended, O'Malley turned to Duchess and the kittens. "Thanks for the best birthday I ever had! It's over now, right?" he said, laughing.

"Yes," Toulouse whispered sleepily. "Happy birthday to you, Abraham DeLacey Giuseppe Casey Thomas O'Malley!"

Who's Responsible?

Simba was far from home when he met Timon and Pumbaa.

"You okay, kid?" Timon asked.

"I guess so," Simba said with a sigh. Timon and Pumbaa could tell the lion cub was lost, tired, and sad. They invited Simba to join them.

Timon and Pumbaa liked the easy life—no problems, no responsibilities. And they had a motto that summed up their attitude.

"Repeat after me," Timon said. *"Hakuna matata."*

"It means 'no worries,'" Pumbaa explained. When his new friends took

him to their jungle home, Simba was amazed by its beauty.

"You live here?" he asked, impressed.

"We live wherever we want," Timon said.

Simba liked his new friends' carefree way of living. They

didn't care about where he was from or why he'd run away. And that was

just fine with Simba.

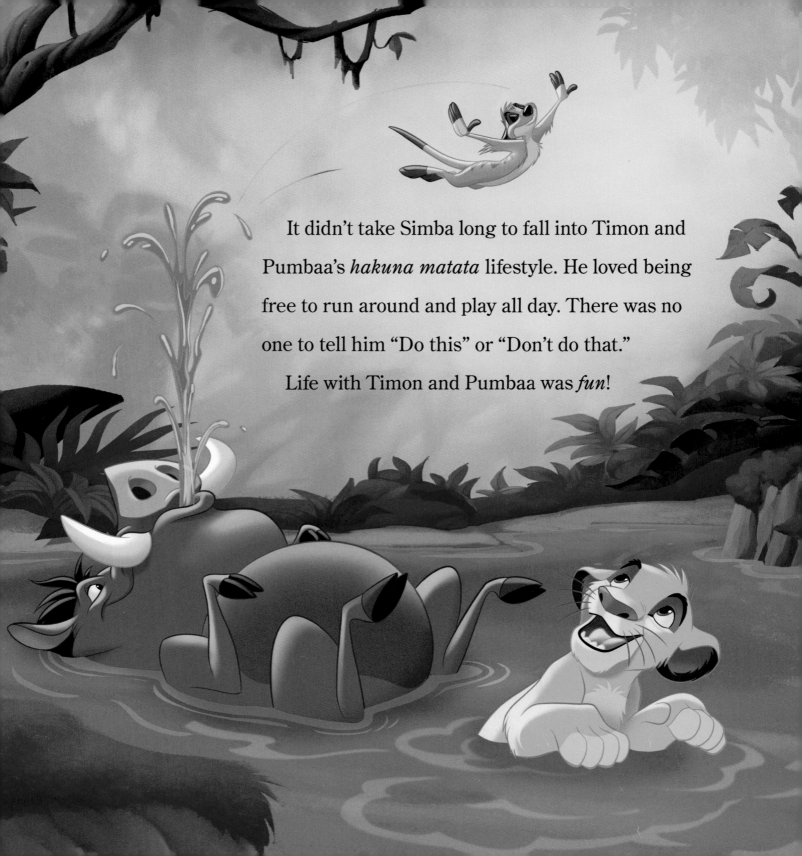

It didn't take Simba long to fall into Timon and Pumbaa's *hakuna matata* lifestyle. He loved being free to run around and play all day. There was no one to tell him "Do this" or "Don't do that."

Life with Timon and Pumbaa was *fun*!

When Simba and his new friends came across a big mud puddle, Simba was the first to jump in.

"This is great!" he shouted. He could get as muddy as he wanted and didn't have to take a bath. No worries!

Pumbaa jumped in, too, splattering mud everywhere.

"Whoa, nice one, Pumbaa," Timon said, laughing.

After a full day of playing in the mud, eating bugs, and living like Timon and Pumbaa, it was time for bed.

While Pumbaa slept, Simba and Timon stayed up, telling jokes and funny stories. Then Timon stood up and yawned.

"Well, that's it for me, kid," he said, climbing into his hammock. "I'm beat. Good night." Within moments, he was fast asleep.

Pumbaa and Timon snored loudly. Simba was having so much fun trying to catch fireflies, he didn't mind that his friends had fallen asleep.

Simba was too excited to go to bed. The jungle looked and sounded so different at night. It felt magical, and he wanted to be a part of it! Besides, he was sure he'd be fine in the morning no matter how late he stayed awake.

The sleepy cub chased fireflies and watched the moon and the stars. He had fun meeting animals who stayed awake at night and slept during the day. At last, he stumbled home and fell asleep.

The next morning Timon and Pumbaa tapped Simba on the shoulder to wake him up. The young lion groaned.

Timon and Pumbaa wanted to go to the water hole, and Simba was grumpy. The water hole was a great place to meet friends. But all the other animals kept their distance from Simba.

"I hate to say this, kid, but you need a bath!" Timon blurted out.

"What do you mean?" asked Simba.

"I know a lot about this," Pumbaa said. "And the fact is, Simba, you stink."

"No way," Simba insisted. "I don't smell a thing."

"But we do, kid. Take a look," Timon said, pointing at the other animals. "No one is standing downwind."

Simba was upset. *Hakuna matata* was supposed to mean no worries and no responsibilities. It wasn't supposed to be about when to take a bath or go to bed or eat dinner!

When they left the water hole, Simba seemed very sad. "I feel like I don't fit in here," he said.

"We understand about not fitting in," said Pumbaa in a kind voice.

"Sorry, kid," Timon added. "That's not what we wanted to happen."

"No, it's not," said Pumbaa. "Before you came here, somebody probably told you what to do all day long."

"Now you gotta do that for yourself," Timon continued.

Suddenly, Pumbaa had an idea. "Hey, we can help you learn about responsibility by being responsible ourselves!" It sounded good to Simba.

"Can we give it a try?" Simba asked. Timon looked at his friends and agreed.

Timon and Pumbaa took Simba to one of their favorite places for a bath. Simba splashed for a bit and then washed off the grime. "It does feel good to get all that dirt off me," he admitted.

"You'll smell better, too," Timon said.

Pumbaa's stomach rumbled. "And taking a bath makes you hungry!"

"Well, come on, then," Timon said. "Let's eat!"

The friends went to a place where several trees had fallen. Simba began trailing a plump beetle.

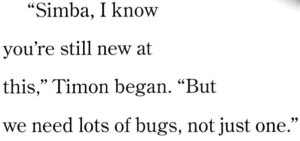

"Simba, I know you're still new at this," Timon began. "But we need lots of bugs, not just one."

"I know," Simba replied. "I'm just following a hunch."

"Pretty sure that's a beetle," joked Timon.

When the beetle scurried under a rotten log, Simba and Pumbaa worked together to break it open.

"Look at that," gasped Timon. "A big, beautiful buffet!"

After dinner, Timon made a bag out of a leaf. He explained, "I'm gonna save some bugs so we'll have something to snack on later."

"Great idea!" said Pumbaa. Working together to make sure there was enough food meant no one would go hungry.

Timon, Pumbaa, and Simba found a nice place to lie down and go to sleep for the night. Timon was fidgety and couldn't seem to get comfortable.

"I need some water," he said. Then, after getting a drink and lying back down, he said, "Ah, still thirsty."

After a few repeats of that, Pumbaa finally said, "Timon! Go. To. Bed."

"Okay, okay," Timon said. "But I'll never fall asleep if I'm still thirsty."

Moments after he lay down, however, Timon was snoring.

Simba smiled. *If Timon can do it, I can do it,* he thought. Then he closed his eyes and drifted off to sleep.

He dreamed of the fun day he'd had with his friends and of all the adventures he would have with them in the future. He slept well knowing he would be happy living with Timon and Pumbaa.

Over the next days, the friends realized something important. Working together, encouraging each other, and setting up routines really did make their lives better. Simba, Timon, and Pumbaa felt great.

The three friends lived their carefree way of life for a very long time. They still had their motto, but they added a little twist: living problem-free . . . responsibly! *Hakuna matata!*

Disney
Peter Pan

Nana and the Game of Hide-and-Seek

It was a rainy afternoon in London, and the Darling children stared out the window at the gray sky. Mother and Father had already left for their evening out.

"Rain, again?" whined Michael, the youngest.

"It's been like this for weeks!" said John, the middle child.

"Now, boys! I know the rain is terribly dull," said Wendy, the oldest and most sensible of the three, "but let's use our imaginations. Nana, what do you think we should do?"

Nana was the Darling children's beloved nanny . . . and dog!

"Woof!" said Nana.

"But I don't want to play a board game. It's boring!" said Michael.

"Woof?" asked Nana.

"Nana, you're the only one who thinks it's fun to try to catch mice in the house," said John.

"Woof, woof," suggested Nana. The children perked up.

"Brilliant idea, Nana! We will all play hide-and-seek," Wendy declared.

"I'll go first!" said Wendy. "You all turn around and count to twenty. When you're finished, come and find me."

"One, two, three . . ." John and Michael said in unison.

"Woof, woof, woof . . ." said Nana.

"Twenty!" the boys shouted.

"Woof!" Nana was ready to seek.

Wendy thought she had found the perfect hiding place.

But the boys and Nana found her easily.

"Found you!" John said, laughing.

"Wendy, why did you hide there?" asked Michael. "How silly!"

"Now it's my turn to hide," said John, already thinking about where to go. "I'll be sure to find a better hiding place than you did, Wendy!"

"Don't be so sure of it," she grumbled.

Nana started the next countdown. *"Woof, woof, woof . . ."*

With all the great hiding spots in the house, John couldn't decide which one to choose.

"Should I hide here?

"Or here?

"Or how about this cupboard? Or . . ."

John spent so much time running from one hiding place to the next that the second round of hide-and-seek turned into a giant game of chase!

"We got you!" Michael squealed with delight. "My turn now! I know the perfect hiding spot, and I want Nana to come with me."

"Woof?" Nana asked.

Nana and Michael went off to hide while the other two children began to count.

Michael and Nana crept out of the nursery and bounded through the hall. Michael led the way to a flight of stairs. Nana had never gone above the floor where the nursery was, and she didn't think Michael had, either.

But up, up, up they went. John and Wendy continued to count.

"The attic!" said Michael proudly, pointing to an old-looking wooden door. "They'll never find us up here. We're sure to win!"

Michael pushed open the heavy door, and Nana pranced in, delighted to be part of the winning plan.

Bang! The door shut behind them.

"Wow!" Michael gasped.

Michael and Nana could not believe their eyes. The attic contained treasure beyond their wildest dreams!

"Look at all of this amazing stuff, Nana!" cried Michael.

"Woof, woof!" Nana agreed.

They tried on all the clothes and played with all the toys they found. It was so much fun!

Meanwhile, Wendy and John were looking everywhere for Michael and Nana. They grew worried as the sun began to set and they still hadn't found them.

"Where are Wendy and John?" asked Michael. He was afraid of the dark, and his voice wobbled. "It's almost nighttime. Why haven't they come to get us yet?"

Nana began to howl. Michael did, too.

"Wendy! John! We're up here!" he shouted.

"Woof! Woof! Woof!" Nana barked as loud as she could.

"Do you hear that, John?" asked Wendy.

"I think it's Nana's bark, coming from upstairs," said John. "Let's go!"

"Oh, you poor things," Wendy said, hearing Michael's and Nana's howling from outside the attic. "John, open the door."

John tried the handle, but it wouldn't turn. Then he began pushing against the door as hard as he could. But the door wouldn't budge.

"I can't—it's locked!" he said.

Locked? Nana suddenly remembered something she had seen in a box.

"Oh, Nana, you lovely old thing," said Michael. "Of course, the keys!"

Nana slipped the keys, one by one, under the door to Wendy and John . . .

. . . who tried each key until they found the one that worked. Wendy and John flung open the door, and all four of them met in a giant hug.

"I think we won the game!" declared Michael, and the others burst into laughter.

Then all three Darling children cheered for their beloved Nana, who had saved the day.

Mowgli's
Great Story

As the moon rose in the sky, Akela finished his nightly story. Mowgli and his wolf brothers burst into howls of approval. Akela was the pack's best storyteller. He wove tales of humor and suspense that kept Mowgli and the cubs hanging on his every word.

"Please, Akela," Mowgli begged. "Won't you tell us one more?"

Akela smiled kindly at the pack. "Not tonight," he replied. "It's past your bedtimes." Sighing, Mowgli and the rest of the cubs scampered off to bed, chattering about the story Akela had told.

The next day, Bagheera brought exciting news to the wolf pack. "In three sunsets, there will be a jungle story contest," he announced.

"What's that?" asked Mowgli, excited.

"It is a chance for the jungle animals to gather and share their best stories," Bagheera explained.

"You have to enter, Akela!" said Mowgli's older wolf brother, Pashu.

Akela shook his head and smiled. "Not this time, young ones," he said. "It is about time you all learned how to tell stories of your own."

Soon word of the contest spread through the jungle. Everywhere Mowgli looked, he saw animals practicing their tales.

Mowgli wanted to share a great story. He wanted it to be funny, scary, mysterious, and full of adventure and bravery.

But the more Mowgli thought about it, the sadder he became. He couldn't seem to come up with a story to tell.

Bagheera could see that Mowgli was struggling. "Let's go for a walk," he said. "Perhaps you will find your story in the jungle."

"How am I going to find my story out here?" Mowgli asked, confused.

"Many of the best stories come from your own life," Bagheera explained. "Look around you for ideas."

As the friends walked through the jungle, Mowgli paid close attention to everything they passed. He heard a woodpecker tap-tap-tapping on a tree. He could tell a story about a bird with a big beak . . . but then what? He saw a turtle paddling through a small river and wondered if he could tell a tale about a brave turtle. But what would happen next?

"Bagheera, I still can't think of anything!" Mowgli said.

"Like a tree waiting to blossom, you must have patience," said Bagheera calmly.

Mowgli groaned and kicked his foot in the dirt. He wondered if he would *ever* come up with an idea.

On the day of the contest, everyone was excited about their stories.

"I'm going to get really quiet at the scary parts and use my *spooooky* voice so everyone gets the shivers," the wolf cub Gray said.

"Just wait until you hear my ending," Pashu said excitedly.

Mowgli sat quietly. He still hadn't come up with a story.

As the sun began to sink in the sky, the jungle animals gathered together to share their tales.

Bagheera began the contest with a fable about patience. Mowgli could tell the story was directed at him. But hearing it didn't make him feel any better about not having his own story to share.

When Bagheera finished his tale, he invited the smallest wolf onto the stage. Gray did an excellent job of telling his story. His spooky voice worked well, and everyone jumped at the right parts!

Next a monkey shared a
silly story about a banana and
a prickly pear. The animals
laughed until their bellies ached.

Pashu shared his story
next. As he had predicted,
everyone was completely
surprised by the ending!

As the animals continued sharing their tales, Mowgli grew more and more nervous. What story was he going to tell?

Chk-chk-chk-chkiii.

Suddenly, Mowgli heard a strange noise coming from deep in the jungle. *Maybe that will lead me to my story,* he thought. Looking around to make sure no one was watching, he quietly slipped away to investigate the sound.

Back at the storytelling contest, a long spotted snake dropped down from his hiding place high in a tree. It was Kaa the python!

"I, too, have a *ssssstory* to share," Kaa hissed.

"Now wait just a minute," Bagheera said, moving toward the snake. But before Bagheera could take another step, Kaa's eyes grew wide, hypnotizing the panther. One by one, everyone fell silent as they stared at the python.

Meanwhile, as Mowgli headed farther into the jungle, he heard the sound again. *Chk-chk-chk-CHKIII!* It was coming from beneath a rock! *What could be under there?* Mowgli wondered, imagining a surprise ending to his story. But when he lifted the rock, he found . . . a bug. The sound had been nothing but a trapped clicking beetle. *Another boring story,* Mowgli thought. With a heavy sigh, he scooted the bug along with his finger and set the rock down.

As he headed back toward the contest, Mowgli tried to think of a way to change the story. *Maybe instead of a beetle it's a . . . fierce tiger,* he thought. He tried to work the tale out in his mind, but he couldn't get it quite right.

Suddenly, Mowgli realized that the jungle had grown oddly quiet. Pushing his way through a bush, he saw that everyone at the contest was sitting completely still. Mowgli looked toward the stage. Kaa was hanging down from a tree. He had all the jungle animals hypnotized!

Mowgli knew he had to act fast. He quietly snuck up the tree and twisted a vine around Kaa's coils. Then he jumped down, rustling the leaves as he landed.

"Who is that?" Kaa yelled, whipping his head around. As he tried to move, the vine tugged him in the opposite direction and snapped him back. His head smacked right into the tree. "My *sssinusssesss*!" he yelped.

Mowgli ran around, clapping his hands together loudly to wake the other animals.

"What's going on?" Bagheera asked Mowgli sleepily.

"Kaa," said Mowgli, pointing to the tree.

"Kaa!" Bagheera's voice boomed.

"Bagheera," Kaa said. "I wasss *jusssst* leaving."

Kaa tried to slither away, but he was still tangled in the vine. With one last big tug, his coils snapped free—and he got twisted up like a pretzel!

As Kaa slowly squirmed back into the jungle brush, Mowgli chuckled to himself. At last, he had found his story.

Mowgli stepped onto the stage and took a deep breath. "Once there was a Man-cub," he began.

Mowgli's story about his life was everything he had wanted it to be: funny, scary, mysterious, and full of adventure and bravery. And that was just what he needed to win the contest!

The Birthday Wish

"Good night, my loves," Duchess said. Her tail swished softly as she gave each of her kittens—Berlioz, Toulouse, and Marie—a tender nuzzle.

"Sleep tight, kiddos," O'Malley said as he tucked them in.

Berlioz and Toulouse purred happily, but Marie didn't want to go to bed.

"Please may I go to the party tonight?" she asked. "I promise to be very good!"

Duchess smiled and shook her head. "Scat Cat will have other birthday parties you can go to when you're older. For now, you need a good night's sleep."

Duchess and O'Malley left and shut the door quietly behind them.

Marie listened as Berlioz began to snore softly. Then Toulouse's whiskers began twitching. Soon both her brothers were fast asleep.

But Marie was wide awake.

Voices drifted from downstairs, then music. Duchess and O'Malley were throwing a birthday party for their friend Scat Cat. He was a jazz musician who had helped Duchess and the kittens when they were separated from their owner.

Marie sighed. Oh, how she wished she were allowed to join them! Why, Scat Cat was her friend, too. It wasn't fair!

After all, Marie could laugh and dance and sing as well as any grown-up.

That's it! Marie thought. She could sneak into the party if she looked like an adult. Tiptoeing carefully, she made her way down the stairs. The coat closet would be full of things she could use to disguise herself!

The noise from the ballroom became louder as Marie slipped into the dark closet. She rummaged around, trying things on. The feather boa tickled her nose. The frilly bonnet wasn't glamorous enough for a party. The dark glasses made it impossible for Marie to see anything.

Finally, she found the perfect disguise. Marie thought she looked very grown-up.

Marie crept into the parlor and looked around. Scat Cat was leading the band in a fast-paced jazz number. Duchess and O'Malley were chatting with some cats in the corner. But most of the cats were dancing. They danced on the floor, on the tables—there was even a cat swinging from the chandelier!

Marie wanted to dance, too. "But I have to stay quiet," she reminded herself. "I musn't get caught!"

"This is a beautiful house," someone said. Marie turned around to see a lady cat wearing a sparkly collar. She was talking to Marie.

"Thank you," Marie said. Then she slapped a paw over her mouth. She was in disguise as a guest. No one could know this was her house!

"I mean," Marie added in a hurry, "I think so, too."

The lady cat gave Marie a funny look. Marie decided to change the subject, fast.

"I like your collar," she said.

"I like your hat," the cat said. Marie beamed. It was working! Her disguise was *perfect*.

Nearby, a cat in an apron appeared, carrying a large platter. "Who wants tuna ice cream?" he said.

"I do! I do!" Marie raised her paw and jumped up and down. Then she remembered—she was supposed to act like a grown-up tonight!

The aproned cat handed her a bowl. "Thank you very much, young fellow," Marie said in her best adult voice. As she tasted the ice cream, she purred loudly. Tuna was her favorite!

Later, some of the guests played party games. Marie enjoyed the charades, but Pin the Tail on the Doggie was her favorite. She won every round!

As Marie removed her blindfold, the band started playing a new tune. Scat Cat put his trumpet down.

"You're on your own, fellas!" he said to the band. "This birthday cat has got a date with the dance floor." Scat Cat walked over to Marie. "Ma'am," he said with a wink, "may I have this dance?"

Marie forget all about getting in trouble. She put her little paw in his, and Scat Cat led her out onto the dance floor.

"Enjoying the party, Marie?" Scat Cat asked.

"Oh, yes!" Marie replied. Then she gasped. "I mean . . . who's Marie?" she asked, trying to cover up her mistake.

"Don't worry. Your secret is safe with me," Scat Cat said. "Let's just dance!"

The music swelled, and Marie took Scat Cat's advice. Then, as the piano trilled, Scat Cat spun her around like a top. Marie whirled—and her disguise went flying off!

"Marie!"

The music stopped, and everyone stared. Marie's disguise was gone, and her mother was marching right toward her!

"Young lady, you are supposed to be in bed!" Duchess said.

Marie looked up sadly. "I'm sorry, Mama," she said. "I didn't mean to disappoint you." Marie felt terrible for making her mother angry.

"Hey now," said a rumbly voice. Marie looked up. It was Scat Cat!

"Say, Duchess, it is my birthday," Scat Cat said, "and Marie's my friend. How about letting her stay?" Scat Cat leaned over toward the birthday cake on the table. "It's my birthday wish!" he said. Then he blew out all the candles and winked at Marie. She smiled back.

Duchess sighed, looking closely at Marie and Scat Cat. "Well, just this once, I suppose. But you are going to bed early tomorrow night, Marie. Understood?"

Marie nodded happily. "Thank you, Mama! I promise I'll never sneak out again."

So Marie stayed at the party, singing and dancing and talking
with the grown-ups. Finally, it was time for everyone to go home. Marie was
as sleepy as she had ever been. As Duchess carried her up to bed, Marie
heard Scat Cat call, "Thanks for coming to my party, Marie!"

"Happy birthday, Scat Cat!" Marie called back. "Thank you for the dance!"

Marie couldn't stop smiling as Duchess tucked her back into bed with her
brothers. She would never forget her special night—or Scat Cat's birthday
wish!

The Pajama Party

Wart couldn't sleep. Ever since Merlin the wizard had arrived, Wart's life had been upside down. Merlin insisted on turning Wart into different animals to enhance Wart's educational experiences—and that was on top of all his normal chores. It was a lot to handle.

That night, the boy looked out his window and saw that the light in Merlin's rickety tower was still on.

Wart paid Merlin a visit. When he arrived, he found that Merlin's owl, Archimedes, was even grumpier than normal. He couldn't sleep. "It's too drafty!" Archimedes said. "It's leaky. It smells weird!"

"Go to *sleep*, you wretched creature!" Merlin shouted.

"Sleep? In this unsuitable environment?" Archimedes huffed.

"You can't sleep, either?" Wart asked.

"I should say not!" Archimedes hooted.

Merlin collapsed into his armchair. "Blasted bird refuse to cooperate," he complained.

"Here," Merlin said, waving his wand. A gigantic book wafted toward Wart. "This one is very boring. Give it a read. It can be part of your bedtime routine."

"What's a bedtime routine?" Wart asked.

Realizing Wart had another important lesson to learn, Merlin jumped up. "Since nobody is getting any sleep, we might as well have a party."

Archimedes eyed the wizard suspiciously. Merlin waved his wand again, and presto change-o . . .

. . . Wart was wearing pajamas! Having never had real pajamas before, he was delighted.

"What is the meaning of this?" Archimedes demanded. "Just because I'm wearing a hat with a tassel does not mean I'm going to bed."

"No, of course not," Merlin scoffed. "We're just having a party. A pajama party!"

"What do we do at a pajama party?" Wart asked.

"Usually there's a story," Merlin said, raising his wand again. "Ribbitus-Rabbitus!" he shouted.

POOF!

Wart could tell something was different.

He shook his head and felt a bit confused.

His long ears flopped. Wait—long ears?

"We're rabbits!" Wart exclaimed.

"The best storyteller around is Mama Rabbit," Merlin explained. "Come on! We'll be late!"

Wart hopped after the wizard, and Archimedes kept pace above as they made their way into the woods.

Soon Merlin skidded to a stop. "We're here," he said, pointing to the entrance of a burrow. "Archimedes, I'm afraid you'll need to listen from a distance."

"Why?" Wart asked.

"It's part of the tension between predators and prey, my boy. You see, some owls eat rabbits. Of course, Archimedes here wouldn't. But it's safer for everyone if Archimedes stays away."

Archimedes rolled his eyes.

Merlin and Wart squeezed themselves through a tunnel and eventually settled near the back of the burrow. The home was filled with young bunnies, all listening intently to Mama Rabbit. Merlin muttered a spell so that he and Wart could understand what she was saying.

Mama Rabbit's voice was gentle, and as she spoke, Wart could see the story unfolding.

"Those little bunnies found their way home," Mama Rabbit said, "and soon after, they fell fast asleep."

Wart yawned. Merlin was already snoring softly next to him.

"Ever since that day," Mama Rabbit said, her voice barely a whisper, "we bunnies have told the story of the—"

"Owl!" a bunny screamed.

Suddenly, everyone in the burrow was *very awake*. There, peeking out from behind his rabbit friends, was Archimedes.

"You didn't really expect me to wait outside, did you? I could barely hear the story," the owl confessed.

"*Get out!*" Mama Rabbit shrieked at the uninvited guests. Her bunnies quickly joined in.

"Merlin! Do something!" Wart cried.

Foomp!

As the smoke cleared, Wart realized he was back in Merlin's tower. He touched his head. The long ears were gone. "I'm a boy again," Wart said.

"And we're back home," Archimedes added. "Not a moment too soon."

Merlin prepared a tray with a pitcher and three cups. "Here we go," he said, spinning around triumphantly. "Warm milk."

As the trio moved to the table, Wart found himself thinking about Mama Rabbit's story. He noticed how soft his new pajamas were. And he suddenly felt very dozy. "You know—" Wart began.

"Shhh," Merlin replied. He pointed at Archimedes, who had fallen asleep. Wart stifled a giggle.

Merlin settled
Archimedes in
his birdhouse and drew a
blanket over his shoulders.

Wart stretched and yawned.
He was ready for bed, too.

With a final wave of his wand, Merlin whisked them back to Wart's room.

The boy climbed into his bed—which had never felt softer in his whole life.

"It's funny," Wart said. "Before this party, I wasn't sleepy at all."

Merlin smiled knowingly. "Comfy pajamas, a bedtime story, and a cup of warm milk," he said. "This, my boy, is a bedtime routine."

Merlin asked, "Do you think you might try it on your own tomorrow night?"

But he got no answer. Wart was fast asleep.

Disney
101 DALMATIANS
Detective Lucky

A blustery wind was blowing outside, but the Dalmatian
puppies—all ninety-nine of them—were snug and
cozy in their new house. The puppies crowded around Nanny,
who was reading them a bedtime story.

Lucky loved bedtime stories. He especially loved ones about detectives!
He wished *he* could be a detective.

When Nanny's story was over, Pongo and Perdita tucked the puppies into bed. But Lucky wasn't tired—not even a little bit! He couldn't stop thinking about all the mysteries he would solve if he were a detective.

One by one, the other puppies drifted off to sleep. Soon Lucky was the only one still awake. Suddenly, his ears twitched.

Creak, squeak, BANG!

What was that strange sound? Lucky bolted upright. Maybe this was it—the mystery he had wished for. Maybe the sound was a clue!

Lucky carefully climbed out of bed. His parents were in the living room with Roger and Anita. No one would notice if Lucky slipped through the doggy door. He could go outside, find some clues, crack the case, and be back before anyone even knew he'd left!

Lucky scampered outside. He looked around. He had never been outside alone at night. The wind had died down, but it was very dark. All around him, Lucky saw strange shadowy shapes.

Lucky thought about going back inside. But he knew that a true detective would solve his case no matter what. If he wanted to be a detective, he'd have to go on, dark or no dark.

Lucky sniffed the air. An unfamiliar smell made his nose twitch. Maybe it was another clue!

Lucky pressed his nose down to the dirt and sniffed again. There it was—the same smell! He wagged his tail as he followed the scent into the woods.

This is exactly what a real detective would do! Lucky thought eagerly as he tracked the smell to a hollow log. Lucky poked his head into the log to see what was inside—and found two spooky eyes staring back at him!

Lucky yelped in surprise. He backed
out of the log as quickly as he could.
Strange noises filled the air, and
Lucky felt something brush by his head.

Hoo-hoo-hoo-hoo!

Flap-flap-flap-whoooooooosh!

Lucky was surrounded by spooky
sounds, and he didn't know what was
making any of them. And even worse,
he'd been so busy tracking the
smell that he hadn't noticed
how far he'd roamed. He
had no idea where he was
going or how to get home!
There was only one
thing to do. Run!

Lucky raced through the forest, ducking under branches and leaping over rocks. When the trees began to thin, he charged forward, running faster and faster until—*wham!* He knocked right into someone!

In a flurry of fur and tails and hisses and growls, Lucky and the stranger tumbled over and over and over. Then the puppy heard a familiar voice: "Lucky? Is that you?"

It was Sergeant Tibs, the cat who'd helped rescue Lucky and his siblings from Cruella De Vil!

"Sergeant Tibs!" Lucky cried in relief. "Help! I'm lost and I don't know how to get home!"

Sergeant Tibs knew just what to do. He led Lucky to an old barn, where the two filled in the Colonel on Lucky's situation.

"This calls for the Midnight Bark!" the Colonel said.

The Colonel lumbered over to the door and howled into the night. Lucky waited anxiously for a response. At last, it came!

Bark! Bark! Bark!

Yip! Yip-yip! Yip, yip, yip!

Arf, arf, arooooo!

The barks echoed across the countryside to the Dalmatians' farm, where a sleepy Pongo opened his eyes.

"It's a lost pup," he whispered to Perdita. "I'll go help."

"Follow the barks. They'll lead you home again," the Colonel told Lucky. "Good luck, lad!"

"Thank you," Lucky told the Colonel and Sergeant Tibs. Then, listening closely, he ran into the night. The Colonel was right. Following the sound of the barks, Lucky soon realized he was on the way home. And now that he was less scared, Lucky was able to solve all the mysteries he'd stumbled upon—even the creaky old gate that had started it all.

Back at the Dalmatian Plantation, Pongo was shocked to see Lucky bounding up to him. "The Midnight Bark was for *you*?" he asked.

"Dad! Dad! I solved a mystery!" Lucky exclaimed. "Just like a real detective!"

"Tell me about it in the morning," Pongo whispered as he led Lucky back to bed. "And no more mysteries tonight!"

Lucky agreed and snuggled up next to his siblings, ready to fall asleep after his big adventure. Suddenly, his ears twitched.

Cro-a-a-a-a-a-k-squeak!

What was that strange sound?

Maybe it was a clue!